CHRISTMAS AT THOMPSON HALL

Christmas
at Thompson Hall
-A Mid-Victorian Christmas Tale-

By

ANTHONY TROLLOPE

ILLUSTRATED

Preface by John Kingsley Shannon

**Caledonia
Press** ❂

Published as a volume in the Harting
Grange Library Series

ISBN 0-932282-07-5 (hardcover trade)
      0-932282-08-3 (softcover)
      0-932282-09-1 (library binding)

LC Card Catalog Number 78-68078

Printed in United States of America

Caledonia Press
P.O. Box 245
Racine, Wisconsin
53401 U.S.A.

123456789

CONTENTS

ILLVSTRATIONS

Preface

Anthony Trollope wrote *Christmas at Thompson Hall* in 1876. This was the year that saw publication of Mark Twain's *Tom Sawyer;* it was the year Alexander Graham Bell patented the telephone; it was also America's Centenary.

When he wrote it, Trollope was sixty-one years old. By then he had published thirty-three novels, as well as a dozen books of essays, travel and such. His first novel *The Macdermots* appeared in 1847, but it wasn't until 1852, with the publication of *The Warden* (first of the Barchester novels), that Trollope, age 40, gained any attention or success. Concurrent with his writing career, Trollope was with the British Post Office, employed first as a junior clerk in 1834, and rising to a position of authority by the time he retired in 1867. After *Christmas at Thompson Hall,* Trollope lived another six years, dying in 1882,—the same year Charles Darwin died and James Joyce was born.

In the Nineteenth Century almost every magazine had its Christmas "number," as do most of ours today, and many book publishers issued Christmas "annuals," just as our publishers plan their Fall Lists with an eye to Christmas sales.

Certainly Charles Dickens, in 1837, eyed the season as he wrote his first novel *The Pickwick Papers,* which was being published in monthly installments; in the middle of the novel, the Pickwickians are in the midst of Christmas, with Chapter XXVIII titled: "A good-humored Christmas chapter, containing an account of a wedding, and some other sports besides. . . ."

This Christmas chapter was only incidental to *Pickwick Papers* as a whole, while six years later, in 1843, Dickens wrote the enormously popular *A Christmas Carol,* the first of his many Christmas stories. After Dickens' success, what author, magazine or publisher could afford not to produce more Christmas stories?

Certainly not Anthony Trollope. In *Christmas at Thompson Hall* he chose to be light and good-humored, like Dickens in *Pickwick,* and not dark and polemic, as was Dickens in *A Christmas Carol.* Trollope's tale turns on a mistaken identity, on several weaknesses,—humorously portrayed, of human nature, and finally on a terrible, terribly farcical coincidence.

Trollope wrote his *Autobiography* the same year as *Thompson Hall,* though the *Autobiog-*

raphy was published after his death. In it Trollope said: "A Christmas story, in the proper sense, should be the ebullition of some mind anxious to instil others with a desire for Christmas religious thought, or Christmas festivities,— or, better still, with Christmas charity." It is with the latter, with charity, and forgiveness, and good-humor,—and with a marriage! that Trollope's story concludes.

John Kingsley Shannon

[*Christmas at Thompson Hall* was first published in *The Graphic*, Christmas number, December 25, 1876. First book publication in 1877.]

CHRISTMAS AT THOMPSON HALL.

CHAPTER I.

MRS. BROWN'S SUCCESS.

EVERY one remembers the severity of the Christmas of 187–. I will not designate the year more closely, lest I should enable those who are too curious to investigate the circumstances of this story, and inquire into details which I do not intend to make known. That winter, however, was especially severe, and the cold of the last ten days of December was more felt, I think, in Paris than in any part of England. It may, indeed, be doubted whether there is any town in any country in which thoroughly bad weather is more afflicting than in the French capital. Snow and hail seem to be colder there, and fires certainly are less warm, than in London. And then there is a feeling among visitors to Paris that Paris ought to be gay; that gayety, prettiness, and liveliness are its aims, as money, commerce, and general business are the aims of London, which, with its

outside sombre darkness, does often seem to
want an excuse for its ugliness. But on this
occasion, at this Christmas of 187–, Paris was
neither gay, nor pretty, nor lively. You could
not walk the streets without being ankle-deep,
not in snow, but in snow that had just become
slush; and there was falling throughout the
day and night of the 23d of December a succession of damp, half-frozen abominations from

the sky which made
it almost impos-
sible for men and
women to go about
their business.

It was at ten
o'clock on that
evening that an
English lady and
gentleman arrived at the Grand Hôtel on the
Boulevard des Italiens. As I have reasons for
concealing the names of this married couple,
I will call them Mr. and Mrs. Brown. Now,
I wish it to be understood that in all the general affairs of life this gentleman and this lady
lived happily together, with all the amenities
which should bind a husband and a wife. Mrs.
Brown was one of a wealthy family, and Mr.

Brown, when he married her, had been relieved
from the necessity of earning his bread.   Nevertheless, she had at once yielded to him when
he expressed a desire to spend the winters of
their life in the South of France ; and he, though
he was by disposition somewhat idle, and but
little prone to the energetic occupations of
life, would generally allow himself, at other
periods of the year, to be carried hither and
thither by her, whose more robust nature de-
lighted in the excitement of travelling.   But on
this occasion there had been a little difference
between them.

Early in December an intimation had reached
Mrs. Brown at Pau that on the coming Christmas there was to be a great gathering of all the
Thompsons in the Thompson family hall at
Stratford-le-Bow, and that she, who had been a
Thompson, was desired to join the party with
her husband.   On this occasion her only sister
was desirous of introducing to the family generally a most excellent young man to whom she
had recently become engaged.   The Thompsons — the real name, however, is in fact con-
cealed — were a numerous and a thriving people.
There were uncles and cousins and brothers
who had all done well in the world, and who

were all likely to do better still. One had
lately been returned to Parliament for the Essex
Flats, and was at the time of which I am writing a conspicuous member of the gallant Con-
servative majority. It was partly in triumph at
this success that the great Christmas gathering
of the Thompsons was to be held, and an opinion had been expressed by the legislator himself
that, should Mrs. Brown, with her husband, fail
to join the family on this happy occasion, she
and he would be regarded as being but *fainéant*
Thompsons.

Since her marriage, which was an affair now
nearly eight years old, Mrs. Brown had never
passed a Christmas in England. The desir-
ability of doing so had often been mooted by
her. Her very soul craved the festivities of
holly and mince-pies. There had ever been
meetings of the Thompsons at Thompson Hall,
though meetings not so significant, not so important to the family, as this one which was
now to be collected. More than once had she
expressed a wish to see old Christmas again in
the old house among the old faces. But her
husband had always pleaded a certain weakness
about his throat and chest as a reason for
remaining among the delights of Pau. Year

after year she had yielded, and now this loud summons had come.

It was not without considerable trouble that she had induced Mr. Brown to come as far as Paris. Most unwillingly had he left Pau; and then, twice on his journey — both at Bordeaux and Tours — he had made an attempt to return. From the first moment he had pleaded his throat, and when at last he had consented to make the journey, he had stipulated for sleeping at those two towns and at Paris. Mrs. Brown, who, with no slightest feeling of fatigue, could have made the journey from Pau to Stratford without stopping, had assented to everything, so that they might be at Thompson Hall on Christmas-eve. When Mr. Brown uttered his unavailing complaints at the first two towns at which they stayed, she did not, perhaps, quite believe all that he said of his own condition. We know how prone the strong are to suspect the weakness of the weak — as the weak are to be disgusted by the strength of the strong. There were, perhaps, a few words between them on the journey, but the result had hitherto been in favor of the lady. She had succeeded in bringing Mr. Brown as far as Paris.

Had the occasion been less important, no

doubt she would have yielded. The weather
had been bad even when they left Pau, but as
they had made their way northward it had
become worse and still worse. As they left
Tours, Mr. Brown, in a hoarse whisper, had
declared his conviction that the journey would
kill him. Mrs. Brown, however, had unfortu-
nately noticed half an hour before that he had
scolded the waiter on the score of an over-
charged franc or two with a loud and clear
voice. Had she really believed that there was
danger, or even suffering, she would have
yielded ; but no woman is satisfied in such a
matter to be taken in by false pretences. She
observed that he ate a good dinner on his way
to Paris, and that he took a small glass of cognac with complete relish, which a man really
suffering from bronchitis surely would not do.
So she persevered, and brought him into Paris,
late in the evening, in the midst of all that
slush and snow. Then, as they sat down to
supper, she thought he did speak hoarsely, and
her loving feminine heart began to misgive her.

But this now was, at any rate, clear to her,—
that he could not be worse off by going on to
London than he would be should he remain in
Paris. If a man is to be ill, he had better be ill

in the bosom of his family than at a hotel. What comfort could he have, what relief, in that huge barrack? As for the cruelty of the weather, London could not be worse than Paris, and then she thought she had heard that sea air is good for a sore throat. In that bedroom which had been allotted to them *au quatrieme* they could not even get a decent fire. It would in every way be wrong now to forego the great Christmas gathering when nothing could be gained by staying in Paris.

She had perceived that, as her husband became really ill, he became also more tractable and less disputatious. Immediately after that little glass of cognac he had declared that he would be —— if he would go beyond Paris, and she began to fear that, after all, everything would have been done in vain. But as they went down to supper between ten and eleven he was more subdued, and merely remarked that this journey would, he was sure, be the death of him. It was half past eleven when they got back to their bedroom, and then he seemed to speak with good sense, and also with much real apprehension. " If I can't get something to relieve me, I know I shall never make my way on," he said. It was intended

that they should leave the hotel at half past
five the next morning, so as to arrive at Stratford, travelling by the tidal train, at half past
seven on Christmas-eve. The early hour, the
 long journey, the infamous weather,
the prospect of that horrid gulf
between Boulogne and Folkestone,
would have been as nothing to Mrs.
Brown, had it not been for that
settled look of anguish which had
now pervaded her husband's face.
" If you don't find something to
relieve me, I shall never live through
it," he said again, sinking back into
the questionable comfort of a Paris-
ian hotel arm-chair.

" But, my dear, what can I do?"
she asked, almost in tears, standing over him and caressing him.
He was a thin, genteel-looking
man, with a fine long soft brown
beard, a little bald at the top of
the head, but certainly a genteel-
looking man. She loved him dearly, and in
her softer moods was apt to spoil him with her
caresses. " What can I do, my dearie? You
know I would do anything if I could.   Get into

bed, my pet, and be warm, and then to-morrow morning you will be all right." At this moment he was preparing himself for his bed, and she was assisting him. Then she tied a piece of flannel round his throat, and kissed him, and put him in beneath the bedclothes.

"I'll tell you what you can do," he said, very hoarsely. His voice was so bad now that she could hardly hear him. So she crept close to him, and bent over him. She would do anything if he would only say what. Then he told her what was his plan. Down in the salon he had seen a large jar of mustard standing on a sideboard. As he left the room he had observed that this had not been withdrawn with the other appurtenances of the meal. If she could manage to find her way down there, taking with her a handkerchief folded for the purpose, and if she could then appropriate a part of the contents of that jar, and, returning with her prize, apply it to his throat, he thought that he could get some relief, so that he might be able to leave his bed the next morning at five. "But I am afraid it will be very disagreeable for you to go down all alone at this time of night," he croaked out in a piteous whisper.

"Of course I'll go," said she. "I don't mind

going in the least.   Nobody will bite me "; and she at once began to fold a clean handkerchief. " I won't be two minutes, my darling; and if there is a grain of mustard in the house, I'll have it on your chest almost immediately." She was a woman not easily cowed, and the journey down into the salon was nothing to her. Before she went she tucked the clothes carefully up to his ears, and then she started.

To run along the first corridor till she came to a flight of stairs was easy enough, and easy enough to descend them.   Then there was another corridor and another flight, and a third corridor and a third flight, and she began to think that she was wrong.   She found herself in a part of the hotel which she had not hitherto visited, and soon discovered by looking through an open door or two that she had found her way among a set of private sitting-rooms which she had not seen before.   Then she tried to make her way back, up the same stairs and through the same passages, so that she might start again.   She was beginning to think that she had lost herself altogether, and that she would be able to find neither the salon nor her bedroom, when she happily met the night porter.   She was dressed in a loose white

dressing-gown, with a white net over her loose
hair, and with white worsted slippers.   I ought,
perhaps, to have described her personal appearance sooner.   She was a large woman with a
commanding bust,
thought by some
to be handsome,
after the manner
of Juno.   But with
strangers there was
a certain severity
of manner about
her — a fortifica-
tion, as it were, of
her virtue against
all possible attacks
—a declared de-
termination to
maintain, at all
points, the beauti-
ful character of a
British matron,
which, much as it
had been appre-
ciated at Thompson Hall, had met with some
ill-natured criticism among French men and
women.   At Pau she had been called La Fière

Anglaise. The name had reached her own
ears and those of her husband. He had been
much annoyed, but she had taken it in good
part — had, indeed, been somewhat proud of
the title — and had endeavored to live up to it.
With her husband she could, on occasion, be
soft, but she was of opinion that with other
men a British matron should be stern. She
was now greatly in want of assistance ; but,
nevertheless, when she met the porter she
remembered her character. " I have lost my
way wandering through these horrid passages,"
she said in her severest tone. This was in
answer to some question from him — some
question to which her reply was given very
slowly. Then, when he asked where madame
wished to go, she paused, again thinking what
destination she would announce. No doubt
the man could take her back to her bedroom,
but if so, the mustard must be renounced, and
with the mustard, as she now feared, all hope
of reaching Thompson Hall on Christmas-eve.
But she, though she was in many respects a
brave woman, did not dare to tell the man that
she was prowling about the hotel in order that
she might make a midnight raid upon the mustard pot. She paused, therefore, for a moment,

that she might collect her thoughts, erecting
her head as she did so in her best Juno fashion,
till the porter was lost in admiration. Thus
she gained time to fabricate a tale. She had,
she said, dropped her handkerchief under the
supper-table; would he show her the way to
the salon, in order that she might pick it up?
But the porter did more than that, and accompanied her to the room in which she had
supped.

Here, of course, there was a prolonged and, it
need hardly be said, a vain search. The good-
natured man insisted on emptying an enormous
receptacle of soiled table napkins, and on turning them over one by one, in order that the
lady's property might be found. The lady
stood by unhappy, but still patient, and as the
man was stooping to his work, her eye was on
the mustard pot. There it was, capable of containing enough to blister the throats of a score
of sufferers. She edged off a little toward it
while the man was busy, trying to persuade
herself that he would surely forgive her if she
took the mustard and told him her whole story.
But the descent from her Juno bearing would
have been so great! She must have owned,
not only to the quest for mustard, but also to a

fib — and she could not do it. The porter was
at last of opinion that madame must have made
a mistake, and madame acknowledged that she
was afraid it was so.

With a longing, lingering eye, with an eye
turned back, oh! so sadly to the great jar, she
left the room, the porter leading the way.   She
assured him that she would find it by herself,
but he would not leave her till he had put her
on to the proper passage.   The journey seemed
to be longer now even than before; but as she
ascended the many stairs she swore to herself
that she would not even yet be balked of her
object.   Should her husband want comfort for
his poor throat, and the comfort be there within
her reach, and he not have it?   She counted
every stair as she went up, and marked every
turn well.   She was sure now that she would
know the way, and that she could return to the
room without fault.   She would go back to the
salon.   Even though the man should encounter her again, she would go boldly forward and
seize the remedy which her poor husband so
grievously required.

"Ah, yes," she said, when the porter told
her that her room, No. 333, was in the corridor
which they had then reached, "I know it all

now. I am so much obliged. Do not come a
step farther." He was anxious to accompany
her up to the very door, but she stood in
the passage, and prevailed. He lingered awhile
— naturally. Unluckily, she had brought no
money with her, and could not give him the
two-franc piece which he had earned. Nor
could she fetch it from her room, feeling that,
were she to return to her husband without the
mustard, no second attempt would be possible.
The disappointed man turned on his heel at
last, and made his way down the stairs and
along the passage. It seemed to her to be
almost an eternity while she listened to his still
audible footsteps. She had gone on, creeping
noiselessly up to the very door of her room,
and there she stood, shading the candle in her
hand, till she thought that the man must have
wandered away into some farthest corner of that
endless building. Then she turned once more
and retraced her steps.

There was no difficulty now as to the way.
She knew it, every stair. At the head of each
flight she stood and listened, but not a sound
was to be heard, and then she went on
again. Her heart beat high with anxious
desire to achieve her object, and at the same

time with fear. What might have been explained so easily at first would now be as difficult of explanation. At last she was in the great public vestibule, which she was now visiting for the third time, and of which, at her last visit, she had taken the bearings accurately. The door was there — closed, indeed, but it opened easily to the hand. In the hall and on the stairs and along the passages there had been gas, but here there was no light beyond that given by the little taper which she carried. When accompanied by the

porter she had not feared the darkness, but now
there was something in the obscurity which
made her dread to walk the length of the
room up to the mustard jar. She paused, and
listened, and trembled. Then she thought of
the glories of Thompson Hall, of the genial
warmth of a British Christmas, of that proud
legislator who was her first cousin, and with
a rush she made good the distance, and laid her
hand upon the copious delf. She looked
round, but there was no one there; no sound
was heard; not the distant creak of a shoe, not
a rattle from one of those thousand doors. As
she paused with her fair hand upon the top of
the jar, while the other held the white cloth on
which the medicinal compound was to be placed,
she looked like Lady Macbeth as she listened
at Duncan's chamber door.

There was no doubt as to the sufficiency of
the contents. The jar was full nearly up to the
lips. The mixture was, no doubt, very different from that good, wholesome English mustard
which your cook makes fresh for you, with a
little water, in two minutes. It was impreg-
nated with a sour odor, and was, to English
eyes, unwholesome of color. But still it was
mustard. She seized the horn spoon, and

without further delay spread an ample sufficiency on the folded square of the handkerchief. Then she commenced to hurry her
return.

But still there was a difficulty, no thought of
which had occurred to her before. The candle
occupied one hand, so that she had but the
other for the sustenance of her treasure. Had
she brought a plate or saucer from the salon,
it would have been all well. As it was, she was
obliged to keep her eye intent on her right
hand, and to proceed very slowly on her return
journey. She was surprised to find what an
aptitude the thing had to slip from her grasp.
But still she progressed slowly, and was careful
not to miss a turning. At last she was safe at
her chamber door. There it was, No. 333.

CHAPTER II.

MRS. BROWN'S FAILURE.

WITH her eye still fixed upon her burden, she glanced up at the number of the door — 333. She had been determined all through not to forget that. Then she turned the latch and crept in. The chamber also was dark after the gaslight on the stairs, but that was so much the better. She herself had put out the two candles on the dressing-table before she had left her husband. As she was closing the door behind her she paused, and could hear that he was sleeping. She was well aware that she had been long absent — quite long enough for a man to fall into slumber who was given that way. She must have been gone, she thought, fully an hour. There had been no end to that turning over of napkins which she had so well known to be altogether vain. She paused at the centre-table of the room, still looking at the mustard, which she now delicately dried from off her hand. She had had no idea that it would have been so difficult to carry so light and so small an affair. But there it was, and nothing had been lost. She took some small instrument from the washing-stand, and with the handle collected the flowing fragments into the centre. Then the question occurred to her whether, as her husband was sleeping so sweetly, it would be well to disturb him. She listened again, and felt that the slight murmur of a snore with which her ears were regaled was altogether free from any real malady in the throat. Then it occurred to her that, after all, fatigue perhaps had only made him cross. She bethought herself how, during the whole journey, she had failed to believe in his illness. What meals he had eaten! How thoroughly he had been able to enjoy his full complement of cigars! And then that glass of brandy, against which she had raised her voice slightly in feminine opposition. And now he was sleeping there like an infant, with full, round, perfected, almost sonorous workings of the throat. Who does not know that sound, almost of two rusty bits of iron scratching against each other, which comes from a suffering windpipe? There was no semblance of that here. Why disturb him when he was so thoroughly enjoying that rest which, more certainly than anything else, would fit him for the fatigue of the morrow's journey?

I think that, after all her labor, she would
have left the pungent cataplasm on the table
and have crept gently into bed beside him, had
not a thought suddenly struck her of the great
injury he had been doing her if he were not
really ill. To send her down there, in a strange
hotel, wandering among the passages, in the
middle of the night, subject to the contumely
of any one who might meet her, on a commis-
sion which, if it were not sanctified by absolute necessity, would be so thoroughly objec-
tionable! At this moment she hardly did
believe that he had ever really been ill. Let
him have the cataplasm; if not as a remedy,
then as a punishment. It could, at any rate, do
him no harm. It was with an idea of avenging
rather than of justifying the past labors of the
night that she proceeded at once to quick
action.

Leaving the candle on the table, so that she
might steady her right hand with the left, she
hurried stealthily to the bedside. Even though
he was behaving badly to her, she would not
cause him discomfort by waking him roughly.
She would do a wife's duty to him as a British
matron should. She would not only put the
warm mixture on his neck, but would sit care-

fully by him for twenty minutes, so that she
might relieve him from it when the proper
period should have come for removing the
counter-irritation from his throat. There would
doubtless be some little difficulty in this — in
collecting the mustard after it had served her
purpose. Had she been at home, surrounded
by her own comforts, the application would
have been made with some delicate linen bag,
through which the pungency of the spice would
have penetrated with strength sufficient for the
purpose. But the circumstance of the occasion
had not admitted this. She had, she felt, done
wonders in achieving so much success as this
which she had obtained. If there should be
anything disagreeable in the operation, he must
submit to it. He had asked for mustard for
his throat, and mustard he should have.

As these thoughts passed quickly through
her mind, leaning over him in the dark, with
her eye fixed on the mixture lest it should slip,
she gently raised his flowing beard with her
left hand, and with her other inverted rapidly,
steadily but very softly fixed the handkerchief
on his throat. From the bottom of his chin to
the spot at which the collar-bones meeting
together form the orifice of the chest, it covered

the whole noble expanse. There was barely
time for a glance, but never had she been
more conscious of the grand proportions of that
manly throat. A sweet feeling of pity came
upon her, causing her to determine to relieve
his sufferings in the shorter space of fifteen
minutes. He had been lying on his back, with
his lips apart, and as she held back his beard,
that and her hand nearly covered the features
of his face. But he made no violent effort to
free himself from the encounter. He did not
even move an arm or a leg. He simply emitted
a snore louder than any that had come before.
She was aware that it was not his wont to be so
loud — that there was generally something more
delicate and perhaps more querulous in his nocturnal voice, but then the present circumstances
were exceptional. She dropped the beard very
softly — and there on the pillow before her lay
the face of a stranger. She had put the mustard plaster on the wrong man.

Not Priam wakened in the dead of night, not
Dido when first she learned that Æneas had
fled, not Othello when he learned that Desde-
mona had been chaste, not Medea when she
became conscious of her slaughtered children,
could have been more struck with horror than

was this British matron as she stood for a moment gazing with awe on that stranger's bed. One vain, half-completed, snatching grasp she made at the handkerchief, and then drew back her hand. If she were to touch him, would he not wake at once, and find her standing there in his bedroom? And then how could she explain it? By what words could she so quickly make him know the circumstances of that strange occurrence that he should accept it all before he had said a word that might offend her? For a moment she stood all but paralyzed after that faint ineffectual movement of her arm. Then he stirred his head uneasily on the pillow, opened wider his lips, and twice in rapid succession snored louder than before. She started back a couple of paces, and with her body placed between him and the candle, with her face averted, but with her hand still resting on the foot of the bed, she endeavored to think what duty required of her.

She had injured the man. Though she had done it most unwittingly, there could be no doubt but that she had injured him. If for a moment she could be brave, the injury might in truth be little; but how disastrous might be the consequences if she were now in her

cowardice to leave him, who could tell? Ap-
plied for fifteen or twenty minutes, a mustard
plaster may be the salvation of a throat ill at
ease; but if left there throughout the night,
upon the neck of a strong man, ailing nothing,
only too prone in his strength to slumber
soundly, how sad, how painful, for aught she
knew how dangerous, might be the effects!
And surely it was an error which any man with
a heart in his bosom might pardon! Judging
from what little she had seen of him, she
thought that he must have a heart in his bosom.
Was it not her duty to wake him, and then
quietly to extricate him from the embarrass-
ment which she had brought upon him?

But in doing this what words should she use?
How should she wake him? How should she
make him understand her goodness, her benefi-
cence, her sense of duty, before he should have
jumped from the bed and rushed to the bell,
and have summoned all above, and all below,
to the rescue? " Sir, sir, do not move, do
not stir, do not scream. I have put a mustard plaster on your throat, thinking that you
were my husband. As yet no harm has been
done. Let me take it off, and then hold your
peace forever." Where is the man of such

native constancy and grace of spirit that, at the
first moment of waking with a shock, he could
hear these words from the mouth of an unknown woman by his bedside, and at once obey
them to the letter? Would he not surely jump
from his bed, with that horrid compound falling
about him — from which there could be no
complete relief unless he would keep his present attitude without a motion. The picture
which presented itself to her mind as to his
probable conduct was so terrible that she found
herself unable to incur the risk.

Then an idea presented itself to her mind.
We all know how in a moment quick thoughts
will course through the subtle brain. She
would find that porter and send him to explain
it all. There should be no concealment now.
She would tell the story and would bid him to
find the necessary aid. Alas! as she told herself that she would do so, she knew well that
she was only running from the danger which it
was her duty to encounter. Once again
she put out her hand as though to return
along the bed. Then thrice he snorted louder
than before, and moved up his knee uneasily beneath the clothes as though the sharp-
ness of the mustard were already working

upon his skin. She watched him for a moment longer, and then, with the candle in her
hand, she fled.

Poor human nature! Had he been an old
man, even a middle-aged man, she would not
have left him to his unmerited sufferings. As
it was, though she completely recognized her
duty, and knew what justice and goodness
demanded of her, she could not do it. But
there was still left to her that plan of sending
the night porter to him. It was not till she
was out of the room and had gently closed the
door behind her that she began to bethink herself how she had made the mistake. With a
glance of her eye she looked up, and then saw
the number on the door — 353. Remarking
to herself, with a Briton's natural criticism on
things French, that those horrid foreigners do
not know how to make their figures, she
scudded rather than ran along the corridor,
and then down some stairs and along another
passage — so that she might not be found in
the neighborhood should the poor man in his
agony rush rapidly from his bed.

In the confusion of her first escape she hardly
ventured to look for her own passage — nor did
she in the least know how she had lost her way

when she came up-stairs with the mustard in
her hand. But at the present moment her
chief object was the night porter. She went on
descending till she came again to that vestibule,
and looking up at the clock saw that it was
now past one. It was not yet midnight when
she left her husband, but she was not at all aston-
ished at the lapse of time. It seemed to her
as though she had passed a night among
these miseries. And, oh, what a night ! But
there was yet much to be done. She must find
that porter, and then return to her own suffering husband. Ah ! what now should she say
to him ? If he should really be ill, how
should she assuage him ? And yet how more
than ever necessary was it that they should
leave that hotel early in the morning — that
they should leave Paris by the very earliest
and quickest train that would take them as
fugitives from their present dangers ! The door
of the salon was open, but she had no courage
to go in search of a second supply. She would
have lacked strength to carry it up the stairs.
Where, now, oh ! where was that man ? From
the vestibule she made her way into the hall,
but everything seemed to be deserted. Through
the glass she could see a light in the court

beyond, but she could not bring herself to endeavor even to open the hall doors.

And now she was very cold — chilled to her
very bones.   All this had been done at Christmas, and during such severity of weather as
had never before been experienced by living
Parisians.   A feeling of great pity for herself
gradually came upon her.   What wrong had
she done, that she should be so grievously
punished?   Why should she be driven to wan-
der about in this way till her limbs were failing
her?   And then so absolutely important as it
was that her strength should support her in the
morning!   The man would not die even though
he were left there without aid, to rid himself of
the cataplasm as best he might.   Was it absolutely necessary that she should disgrace herself?

But she could not even procure the means
of disgracing herself, if that telling her story to
the night porter would have been a disgrace.
She did not find him, and at last resolved to
make her way back to her own room without
further quest.   She began to think that she had
done all that she could do.   No man was ever
killed by a mustard plaster on his throat.   His
discomfort at the worst would not be worse than

hers had been — or, too probably, than that of her poor husband. So she went back up the stairs and along the passages, and made her way on this occasion to the door of her room without any difficulty. The way was so well known to her that she could not but wonder that she had failed before. But now her hands had been empty, and her eyes had been at her full command. She looked up, and there was the number, very manifest on this occasion — 333. She opened the door most gently, thinking that her husband might be sleeping as soundly as that other man had slept, and she crept into the room.

CHAPTER III.

MRS. BROWN ATTEMPTS TO ESCAPE.

BUT her husband was not sleeping.   He was not even in bed, as she had left him.   She found

him sitting there before the fireplace, on which
one half-burned log still retained a spark of
what had once pretended to be a fire. Nothing
more wretched than his appearance could be
imagined. There was a single lighted candle
on the table, on which he was leaning with his
two elbows, while his head rested between his
hands. He had on a dressing-gown over his
nightshirt, but otherwise was not clothed. He
shivered audibly, or rather shook himself with
the cold, and made the table to chatter, as she
entered the room. Then he groaned, and let
his head fall from his hands on to the table. It
occurred to her at the moment, as she recognized
the tone of his querulous voice, and as she saw
the form of his neck, that she must have been
deaf and blind when she had mistaken that stal-
wart stranger for her husband. "O my dear,"
she said, "why are you not in bed?" He
answered nothing in words, but only groaned
again. "Why did you get up? I left you
warm and comfortable."

"Where have you been all night?" he half
whispered, half croaked, with an agonizing effort.

"I have been looking for the mustard."

"Have been looking all night, and haven't
found it? Where have you been?"

She refused to speak a word to him till she had got him into bed, and then she told her story. But, alas! that which she told was not the true story. As she was persuading him to go back to his rest, and while she arranged the clothes again around him, she with difficulty made up her mind as to what she would do and what she would say. Living or dying, he must be made to start for Thompson Hall at half past five on the next morning. It was no longer a question of the amenities of Christmas, no longer a mere desire to satisfy the family ambition of her own people, no longer an anxiety to see her new brother-in-law. She was conscious that there was in that house one whom she had deeply injured, and from whose vengeance — even from whose aspect — she must fly. How could she endure to see that face which she was so well sure that she would recognize, or to hear the slightest sound of that voice which would be quite familiar to her ears, though it had never spoken a word in her hearing? She must certainly fly on the wings of the earliest train which would carry her toward the old house; but in order that she might do so, she must propitiate her husband.

So she told her story. She had gone forth,

as he had bade her, in search of the mustard, and then had suddenly lost her way. Up and down the house she had wandered, perhaps nearly a dozen times. "Had she met no one?" he asked, in that raspy, husky whisper. "Surely there must have been some one about the hotel! Nor was it possible that she could have been roaming about all those hours." "Only one hour, my dear," she said. Then there was a question about the duration of time, in which both of them waxed angry; and as she became angry, her husband waxed stronger, and as he became violent beneath the clothes, the comfortable idea returned to her that he was not perhaps so ill as he would seem to be. She found herself driven to tell him something about the porter, having to account for that lapse of time by explaining how she had driven the poor man to search for the handkerchief which she had never lost.

"Why did you not tell him you wanted the mustard?"

"My dear!"

"Why not? There is nothing to be ashamed of in wanting mustard."

"At one o'clock in the morning! I couldn't do it. To tell you the truth, he wasn't very civil, and I thought that he was — perhaps a little tipsy. Now, my dear, do go to sleep."

"Why didn't you get the mustard?"

"There was none there — nowhere at all about the room. I went down again and searched everywhere. That's what took me so long. They always lock up those kind of things at these French hotels. They are too close-fisted to leave anything out. When you first spoke of it I knew that it would be gone when I got there. Now, my dear, do go to sleep, because we positively must start in the morning."

"That is impossible," said he, jumping up in the bed.

"We must go, my dear. I say that we must go. After all that has passed, I wouldn't not be with Uncle John and my cousin Robert to-morrow evening for more — more — more than I would venture to say."

"Bother!" he exclaimed.

"It's all very well for you to say that, Charles, but you don't know. I say that we must go to-morrow, and we will."

"I do believe you want to kill me, Mary."

"That is very cruel, Charles, and most false, and most unjust. As for making you ill, nothing could be so bad for you as this wretched

place, where nobody can get warm either day
or night. If anything will cure your throat for
you at once, it will be the sea air. And only
think how much more comfortable they can
make you at Thompson Hall than anywhere in
this country. I have so set my heart upon it,
Charles, that I will do it. If we are not there
to-morrow night, Uncle John won't consider us
as belonging to the family."

"I don't believe a word of it."

"Jane told me so in her letter. I wouldn't let
you know before because I thought it so unjust.
But that has been the reason why I've been so
earnest about it all through."

It was a thousand pities that so good a woman
should have been driven by the sad stress of circumstances to tell so many fibs. One after another she was compelled to invent them, that
there might be a way open to her of escaping
the horrors of a prolonged sojourn in that hotel.
At length, after much grumbling, he became
silent, and she trusted that he was sleeping. He
had not as yet said that he would start at the
required hour in the morning, but she was perfectly determined in her own mind that he
should be made to do so. As he lay there
motionless, and as she wandered about the room

pretending to pack her things, she more than once almost resolved that she would tell him everything. Surely then he would be ready to make any effort. But there came upon her an idea that he might perhaps fail to see all the circumstances, and that, so failing, he would insist on remaining that he might tender some apology to the injured gentleman. An apology might have been very well had she not left him there in his misery; but what apology would be possible now? She would have to see him and speak to him, and every one in the hotel would know every detail of the story. Every one in France would know that it was she who had gone to the strange man's bedside and put the mustard plaster on the strange man's throat in the dead of night! She could not tell the story even to her husband, lest even her husband should betray her.

Her own sufferings at the present moment were not light. In her perturbation of mind she had foolishly resolved that she would not herself go to bed. The tragedy of the night had seemed to her too deep for personal comfort. And then, how would it be were she to sleep, and have no one to call her? It was imperative that she should have all her powers ready for thoroughly arousing him. It occurred to her that the servant of the hotel would certainly run her too short of time. She had to work for herself and for him too, and therefore she would not sleep. But she was very cold, and she put on first a shawl over her dressing-gown and then a cloak. She could not consume all the remaining hours of the night in packing one bag and one portmanteau; so that at last she sat down on the narrow red cotton velvet sofa, and, looking at her watch, perceived that as yet it was not much past two o'clock. How was she to get through those other three long, tedious, chilly hours?

Then there came a voice from the bed, — "Ain't you coming?"

"I hoped you were asleep, my dear."

"I haven't been asleep at all. You'd better come, if you don't mean to make yourself as ill as I am."

"You are not so very bad, are you, darling?"

"I don't know what you call bad. I never felt my throat so choked in my life before." Still as she listened she thought that she remembered his throat to have been more choked. If the husband of her bosom could play with her feelings and deceive her on such an occasion as this — then — then — then she thought that she would rather not have any husband of her bosom at all. But she did creep into bed, and lay down beside him without saying another word.

Of course she slept, but her sleep was not the sleep of the blest. At every striking of the clock in the quadrangle she would start up in alarm, fearing that she had let the time go by. Though the night was so short, it was very long to her. But he slept like an infant. She could hear from his breathing that he was not quite so well as she could wish him to be, but still he was resting in beautiful tranquillity. Not once did he move when she started up, as she did so frequently. Orders had been given and repeated over and over again that they should be called at five. The man in the office had almost been angry as he assured Mrs. Brown for the fourth time that monsieur and madame would most assuredly be wakened at the appointed time. But still she would trust to no one, and was up and about the room before the clock had struck half past four.

In her heart of hearts she was very tender toward her husband. Now, in order that he might feel a gleam of warmth while he was dressing himself, she collected together the fragments of half-burned wood, and endeavored to make a little fire. Then she took out from her bag a small pot and a patent lamp and some chocolate, and prepared for him a warm drink, so that he might have it instantly as he was awakened. She would do anything for him in the way of ministering to his comfort —only he must go! Yes, he certainly must go!

And then she wondered how that strange man was bearing himself at the present moment. She would fain have ministered to him too had it been possible; but, ah! it was so impossible! Probably before this he would have been aroused from his troubled slumbers. But then— how aroused? At what time in the night would the burning heat upon his chest have awakened him to a sense of torture which must

have been so altogether incomprehensible to
him? Her strong imagination showed to her
a clear picture of the scene — clear, though it
must have been done in the dark. How he
must have tossed and hurled himself under the
clothes! how those strong knees must have
worked themselves up and down before the
potent god of sleep would allow him to return
to perfect consciousness! how his fingers, re-
strained by no reason, would have trampled
over his feverish throat, scattering everywhere
that unhappy poultice! Then when he should
have sat up wide awake, but still in the dark —
with her mind's eye she saw it all — feeling that
some fire as from the infernal regions had fallen
upon him, but whence he would know not, how
fiercely wild would be the working of his spirit!
Ah, now she knew, now she felt, now she
acknowledged, how bound she had been to
awaken him at the moment, whatever might
have been the personal inconvenience to herself! In such a position what would he do —
or rather what had he done? She could follow
much of it in her own thoughts: how he would
scramble madly from his bed, and, with one
hand still on his throat, would snatch hurriedly
at the matches with the other. How the light

would come, and how then he would rush to
the mirror.   Ah, what a sight he would behold!
She could see it all, to the last wide-spread daub.

But she could not see, she could not tell herself, what in such a position a man would do;
at any rate, not what that man would do.   Her
husband, she thought, would tell his wife, and
then the two of them, between them, would —
put up with it.

There are misfortunes which, if they be published, are simply aggravated by ridicule.   But
she remembered the features of the stranger as
she had seen them at that instant in which she
had dropped his beard, and she thought that
there was a ferocity in them, a certain tenacity
of self-importance, which would not permit their
owner to endure such treatment in silence.
Would he not storm and rage, and ring the
bell, and call all Paris to witness his revenge?

But the storming and the raging had not
reached her yet, and now it wanted but a quarter to five.   In three-quarters of an hour they
would be in that demi-omnibus which they had
ordered for themselves, and in half an hour
after that they would be flying toward Thompson Hall.   Then she allowed herself to think of
those coming comforts — of those comforts so

sweet, if only they would come! That very day now present to her was the 24th December, and on that very evening she would be sitting in Christmas joy among all her uncles and cousins, holding her new brother-in-law affectionately by the hand. Oh, what a change from Pandemonium to Paradise! from that wretched room, from that miserable house in which there was such ample cause for fear, to all the domestic Christmas bliss of the home of the Thompsons! She resolved that she would not, at any rate, be deterred by any light opposition on the part of her husband. "It wants just a quarter to five," she said, putting her hand steadily upon his shoulder, "and I'll get a cup of chocolate for you, so that you may get up comfortably."

"I've been thinking about it," he said, rubbing his eyes with the back of his hands. "It will be so much better to go over by the mail-train to-night. We should be in time for Christmas just the same."

"That will not do at all," she answered, energetically. "Come, Charles, after all the trouble, do not disappoint me."

"It is such a horrid grind."

"Think what I have gone through — what I

have done for you! In twelve hours we shall
be there, among them all. You won't be so
little like a man as not to go on now." He
threw himself back upon the bed, and tried to
re-adjust the clothes around his neck. "No,
Charles, no," she continued; "not if I know it.
Take your chocolate and get up. There is not
a moment to be lost." With that she laid her
hand upon his shoulder, and made him clearly
understand that he would not be allowed to
take further rest in that bed.

Grumbling, sulky, coughing continually, and
declaring that life under such circumstances
was not worth having, he did at last get up and
dress himself. When once she knew that he
was obeying her, she became again tender to
him, and certainly took much more than her
own share of the trouble of the proceedings.
Long before the time was up she was ready,
and the porter had been summoned to take the
luggage down-stairs. When the man came,
she was rejoiced to see that it was not he whom
she had met among the passages during her
nocturnal rambles. He shouldered the box, and
told them that they would find coffee and bread
and butter in the small *salle à manger* below.

"I told you that it would be so, when you

would boil that stuff," said the ungrateful man, who had nevertheless swallowed the hot choco- late when it was given to him.

They followed their luggage down into the hall; but as she went, at every step, the lady looked around her. She dreaded the sight of that porter of the night; she feared lest some potential authority of the hotel should come to her and ask her some horrid question; but of all her fears her greatest fear was that there should arise before her an apparition of that face which she had seen recumbent on its pillow.

As they passed the door of the great salon, Mr. Brown looked in. "Why, there it is still!" said he.

"What?" said she, trembling in every limb.

"The mustard pot."

"They have put it in there since," she ex- claimed, energetically, in her despair. "But never mind. The omnibus is here. Come away." And she absolutely took him by the arm.

But at that moment a door behind them opened, and Mrs. Brown heard herself called by her name. And there was the night porter — with a handkerchief in his hand. But the further doings of that morning must be told in a further chapter.

CHAPTER IV.

MRS. BROWN DOES ESCAPE.

IT had been visible to Mrs. Brown from the first moment of her arrival on the ground floor that "something was the matter," if we may be allowed to use such a phrase; and she felt all but convinced that this something had reference to her. She fancied that the people of the hotel were looking at her as she swallowed, or tried to swallow, her coffee. When her husband was paying the bill there was something disagreeable in the eye of the man who was taking the money. Her sufferings were very great, and no one sympathized with her. Her husband was quite at his ease, except that he was complaining of the cold. When she was anxious to get him out into the carriage, he still stood there, leisurely arranging shawl after shawl around his throat. "You can do that quite as well in the omnibus," she had just said to him, very crossly, when there appeared upon the scene through a side door that very night porter whom she dreaded with a soiled pocket-handkerchief in his hand.

Even before the sound of her own name met her ears, Mrs. Brown knew it all. She understood the full horror of her position from that man's hostile face, and from the little article which he held in his hand. If during the watches of the night she had had money in her pocket, if she had made a friend of this greedy fellow by well-timed liberality, all might have been so different! But she reflected that she had allowed him to go unfeed after all his trouble, and she knew that he was her enemy. It was the handkerchief that she feared. She thought that she might have brazened out anything but that. No one had seen her enter or leave that strange man's  room. No one had seen her dip her hands in that jar. She had, no doubt, been found wandering about the house while the slumberer had been made to suffer so strangely, and there might have been suspicion, and perhaps accu-

sation.   But she would have been ready with
frequent protestations to deny all charges made
against her, and though no one might have
believed her, no one could have convicted her.
Here, however, was evidence against which she
would be unable to stand for a moment.   At the
first glance she acknowledged the potency of
that damning morsel of linen.

During all the horrors of the night she had
never given a thought to the handkerchief, and
yet she ought to have known that the evidence
it would bring against her was palpable and certain.   Her name, "M. Brown," was plainly written on the corner.   What a fool she had been
not to have thought of this!   Had she but remembered the plain marking which she, as a
careful, well-conducted British matron, had put
upon all her clothes, she would at any hazard
have recovered the article.   Oh that she had
waked the man, or bribed the porter, or even
told her husband!   But now she was, as it were,
friendless, without support, without a word that
she could say in her own defence, convicted of
having committed this assault upon a strange
man as he slept in his own bedroom, and then
of having left him!   The thing must be explained by the truth; but how to explain such

truth, how to tell such story in a way to satisfy injured folk, and she with only barely time sufficient to catch the train! Then it occurred to her that they could have no legal right to stop her because the pocket-handkerchief had been found in a strange gentleman's bedroom. "Yes, it is mine," she said, turning to her husband, as the porter, with a loud voice, asked if she were not Madame Brown. "Take it, Charles, and come on." Mr. Brown naturally stood still in astonishment. He did put out his hand, but the porter would not allow the evidence to pass so readily out of his custody.

"What does it all mean?" asked Mr. Brown.

"A gentleman has been — eh — eh — Something has been done to a gentleman in his bedroom," said the clerk.

"Something done to a gentleman!" repeated Mr. Brown.

"Something very bad indeed," said the porter. "Look here"; and he showed the condition of the handkerchief.

"Charles, we shall lose the train," said the affrighted wife.

"What the mischief does it all mean?" demanded the husband.

"Did madame go into the gentleman's

room?" asked the clerk. Then there was an awful silence, and all eyes were fixed upon the lady.

"What does it all mean?" demanded the husband. "Did you go into anybody's room?"

"I did," said Mrs. Brown with much dignity, looking round upon her enemies as a stag at bay will look upon the hounds which are attacking him. "Give me the handkerchief." But the night porter quickly put it behind his back. "Charles, we cannot allow ourselves to be delayed. You shall write a letter to the keeper of the hotel explaining it all." Then she essayed to swim out through the front door into the courtyard, in which the vehicle was waiting for them. But three or four men and women interposed themselves, and even her husband did not seem quite ready to continue his journey. "To-night is Christmas-eve," said Mrs. Brown, "and we shall not be at Thompson Hall. Think of my sister!"

"Why did you go into the man's bedroom, my dear?" whispered Mr. Brown in English.

But the porter heard the whisper, and understood the language—the porter who had not been "tipped." "Ye'es—vy?" asked the porter.

"It was a mistake, Charles; there is not a moment to lose. I can explain it all to you in the carriage." Then the clerk suggested that madame had better postpone her journey a little. The gentleman up-stairs had certainly been very badly treated, and had demanded to know why so great an outrage had been perpetrated. The clerk said that he did not wish to send for the police (here Mrs. Brown gasped terribly, and threw herself on her husband's shoulder), but he did not think he could allow the party to go till the gentleman up-stairs had received some satisfaction. It had now become clearly impossible that the journey could be made by the early train. Even Mrs. Brown gave it up herself, and demanded of her husband that she should be taken back to her bedroom.

"But what is to be said to the gentleman?" asked the porter.

Of course it was impossible that Mrs. Brown should be made to tell her story there in the presence of them all. The clerk, when he found he had succeeded in preventing her from leaving the house, was satisfied with a promise from Mr. Brown that he would inquire from his wife what were these mysterious circumstances, and would then come down to the office and give some explanation. If it were necessary, he would see the strange gentleman — whom he now ascertained to be a certain Mr. Jones, returning from the east of Europe. He learned also that this Mr. Jones had been most anxious to travel by that very morning train which he and his wife had intended to use; that Mr. Jones had been most particular in giving his orders accordingly; but that at the last moment he had declared himself to be unable even to dress himself, because of the injury which had been done him during the night. When Mr. Brown heard this from the clerk just before he was allowed to take his wife up-stairs, while she was sitting on a sofa in a corner with her face hidden, a look of awful gloom came over his own countenance. What could it be that his wife had done to the man, of so terrible a nature? "You had better come up with me," he said to her, with marital severity; and the poor cowed woman went with him tamely as might have done some patient Grizel. Not a word was spoken till they were in the room and the door was locked. "Now," said he, "what does it all mean?"

It was not till nearly two hours had passed that Mr. Brown came down the stairs very slowly, turning it all over in his mind. He had now

gradually heard the absolute and exact truth,
and had very gradually learned to believe it.
It was first necessary that he should understand
that his wife had told him many fibs during the
night; but, as she constantly alleged to him
when he complained of her conduct in this respect, they had all been told on his behalf. Had
she not struggled to get the mustard for his
comfort, and when she had secured the prize
had she not hurried to put it on — as she had
fondly thought — his throat? And though she
had fibbed to him afterward, had she not done
so in order that he might not be troubled?
"You are not angry with me because I was in
that man's room?" she asked, looking full into
his eyes, but not quite without a sob. He
paused a moment, and then declared, with something of a true husband's confidence in his tone,
that he was not in the least angry with her on
that account. Then she kissed him, and bade
him remember that, after all, no one could really
injure them. "What harm has been done,
Charles? The gentleman won't die because he
has had a mustard plaster on his throat. The
worst is about Uncle John and dear Jane. They
do think so much of Christmas-eve at Thompson Hall!"

Mr. Brown, when he again found himself in the clerk's office, requested that his card might be taken up to Mr. Jones. Mr. Jones had sent down his own card, which was handed to Mr. Brown: "Mr. Barnaby Jones." "And how was it all, sir?" asked the clerk, in a whisper — a whisper which had at the same time something of authoritative demand and something also of submissive respect. The clerk, of course, was anxious to know the mystery. It is hardly too much to say that every one in that vast hotel was by this time anxious to have the mystery unravelled. But Mr. Brown would tell nothing to any one. "It is merely a matter to be explained between me and Mr. Jones," he said. The card was taken up-stairs, and after a while he was ushered into Mr. Jones's room. It was, of course, that very 353 with which the reader is already acquainted. There was a fire burning, and the remains of Mr. Jones's breakfast were on the table. He was sitting in his dressing-gown and slippers, with his shirt open in the front, and a silk handkerchief very loosely covering his throat. Mr. Brown, as he entered the room, of course looked with considerable anxiety at the gentleman of whose condition he had heard so sad an account; but he could

only observe some considerable stiffness of
movement and demeanor as Mr. Jones turned
his head round to greet him.

"This has been a very disagreeable accident,
Mr. Jones," said the husband of the lady.

"Accident!   I don't know how it could have
been an accident.   It has been a most — most —
most — a most monstrous — er — er — I must
say, interference with a gentleman's privacy and
personal comfort."

"Quite so, Mr. Jones, but — on the part of the lady, who is my wife —"

"So I understand. I myself am about to become a married man, and I can understand what your feelings must be. I wish to say as little as possible to harrow them." Here Mr. Brown bowed. "But — there's the fact. She did do it."

"She thought it was — me!"

"What!"

"I give you my word as a gentleman, Mr. Jones. When she was putting that mess upon you, she thought it was me! She did indeed."

Mr. Jones looked at his new acquaintance and shook his head. He did not think it possible that any woman would make such a mistake as that.

"I had a very bad sore throat," continued Mr. Brown, "and indeed you may perceive it still" — in saying this he perhaps aggravated a little the sign of his distemper — "and I asked Mrs. Brown to go down and get one — just what she put on you."

"I wish you'd had it," said Mr. Jones, putting his hand up to his neck.

"I wish I had, for your sake as well as mine,

and for hers, poor woman.   I don't know when
she will get over the shock."

"I don't know when I shall.   And it has
stopped me on my journey.   I was to have
been to-night, this very night, this Christmas-
eve, with the young lady I am engaged to
marry.   Of course I couldn't travel.   The ex-
tent of the injury done nobody can imagine
at present."

"It has been just as bad to me, sir.   We
were to have been with our family this Christmas-eve.   There were particular reasons —
most particular.   We were only hindered from
going by hearing of your condition."

"Why did she come into my room at all?   I
can't understand that.   A lady always knows
her own room at a hotel."

"353 — that's yours; 333 — that's ours.
Don't you see how easy it was?   She had lost
her way, and she was a little afraid lest the
thing should fall down."

"I wish it had with all my heart."

"That's how it was.   Now I'm sure, Mr.
Jones, you'll take a lady's apology.   It was a
most unfortunate mistake — most unfortunate;
but what more can be said?"

Mr. Jones gave himself up to reflection for a

few moments before he replied to this. He
supposed that he was bound to believe the
story as far as it went. At any rate, he did
not know how he could say that he did not
believe it. It seemed to him to be almost incredible, especially incredible in regard to that
personal mistake, for, except that they both
had long beards and brown beards, Mr. Jones
thought that there was no point of resemblance
between himself and Mr. Brown. But still,
even that, he felt, must be accepted. But then
why had he been left, deserted, to undergo all
those torments? "She found out her mistake
at last, I suppose?" he said.

"Oh, yes."

"Why didn't she wake a fellow and take it
off again?"

"Ah!"

"She can't have cared very much for a man's
comfort, when she went away and left him like
that."

"Ah! there was the difficulty, Mr. Jones."

"Difficulty! Who was it that had done it?
To come to me in my bedroom in the middle
of the night and put that thing on me, and then
leave it there and say nothing about it! It
seems to me deuced like a practical joke."

"No, Mr. Jones."

"That's the way I look at it," said Mr. Jones, plucking up his courage.

"There isn't a woman in all England or in all France less likely to do such a thing than my wife. She's as steady as a rock, Mr. Jones, and would no more go into another gentleman's bedroom in joke than — Oh dear no! You're going to be a married man yourself."

"Unless all this makes a difference," said Mr. Jones, almost in tears. "I had sworn that I would be with her this Christmas-eve."

"O Mr. Jones, I cannot believe that will interfere with your happiness. How could you think that your wife, as is to be, would do such a thing as that in joke?"

"She wouldn't do it at all, joke or any way."

"How can you tell what accident might happen to any one?"

"She'd have wakened the man, then, afterward. I'm sure she would. She would never have left him to suffer in that way. Her heart is too soft. Why didn't she send you to wake me and explain it all? That's what my Jane would have done; and I should have gone and wakened him. But the whole thing is impossible," he said, shaking his head as he

remembered that he and his Jane were not in a
condition as yet to undergo any such mutual
trouble. At last Mr. Jones was brought to
acknowledge that nothing more could be done.
The lady had sent her apology and told her
story, and he must bear the trouble and inconvenience to which she had subjected him. He
still, however, had his own opinion about her
conduct generally, and could not be brought
to give any sign of amity. He simply bowed
when Mr. Brown was hoping to induce him to
shake hands, and sent no word of pardon to the
great offender.

The matter, however, was so far concluded
that there was no further question of police
interference, nor any doubt but that the lady,
with her husband, was to be allowed to leave
Paris by the night train. The nature of the
accident probably became known to all. Mr.
Brown was interrogated by many, and though
he professed to declare that he would answer
no question, nevertheless he found it better to
tell the clerk something of the truth than to
allow the matter to be shrouded in mystery.
It is to be feared that Mr. Jones, who did not
once show himself through the day, but who
employed the hours in endeavoring to assuage

the injury done him, still lived in the conviction
that the lady had played a practical joke on
him. But the subject of such a joke never
talks about it, and Mr. Jones could not be induced to speak even by the friendly adherence
of the night porter.

Mrs. Brown also clung to the seclusion of her
own bedroom, never once stirring from it till the
time came in which she was to be taken down
to the omnibus. Up-stairs she ate her meals,
and up-stairs she passed her time in packing
and unpacking, and in requesting that telegrams might be sent repeatedly to Thompson
Hall. In the course of the day two such telegrams were sent, in the latter of which the
Thompson family were assured that the Browns
would arrive probably in time for breakfast on
Christmas-day, certainly in time for church.
She asked more than once tenderly after Mr.
Jones's welfare, but could obtain no informa-
tion. "He was very cross, and that's all I
know about it," said Mr. Brown. Then she
made a remark as to the gentleman's Christian
name, which appeared on the card as "Barnaby." "My sister's husband's name will
be Burnaby," she said. "And this man's
Christian name is Barnaby; that's all the

difference," said her husband, with ill-timed
jocularity.

We all know how people under a cloud are
apt to fail in asserting their personal dignity.
On the former day a separate vehicle had been
ordered by Mr. Brown to take himself and his
wife to the station, but now, after his misfortunes, he contented himself with such provision
as the people at the hotel might make for him.
At the appointed hour he brought his wife
down, thickly veiled.   There were many strangers, as she passed through the hall, ready to
look at the lady who had done that wonderful
thing in the dead of night, but none could see
a feature of her face as she stepped across the
hall and was hurried into the omnibus.   And
there were many eyes also on Mr. Jones, who
followed her very quickly, for he also, in spite
of his sufferings, was leaving Paris on the evening in order that he might be with his English
friends on Christmas-day.   He, as he went
through the crowd, assumed an air of great
dignity, to which, perhaps, something was added
by his endeavors as he walked to save his poor
throat from irritation.   He, too, got into the
same omnibus, stumbling over the feet of his
enemy in the dark.   At the station they got

their tickets, one close after the other, and then were brought into each other's presence in the waiting-room. I think it must be acknowledged that here Mr. Jones was conscious not only of her presence, but of her consciousness of his presence, and that he assumed an attitude as though he should have said, "Now do you think it possible for me to believe that you mistook me for your husband?" She was perfectly quiet, but sat through that quarter of an hour with her face continually veiled. Mr. Brown made some little overture of conversation to Mr. Jones, but Mr. Jones, though he did mutter some reply, showed plainly enough that he had no desire for further intercourse. Then came the accustomed stampede, the awful rush, the internecine struggle in which seats had to be found. Seats, I fancy, are regularly found, even by the most tardy, but it always appears that every British father and every British husband is actuated at these stormy moments by a conviction that unless he proves himself a very Hercules he and his daughters and his wife will be left desolate in Paris. Mr. Brown was quite Herculean, carrying two bags and a hatbox in his own hands, besides the cloaks, the coats, the rugs, the sticks, and the umbrellas. But when he had got himself and his wife well seated, with their faces to the engine, with a corner seat for her — there was Mr. Jones immediately opposite to her.   Mr. Jones, as soon as he perceived the inconvenience of his position, made a scramble for another place, but he was too late.   In that contiguity the journey as far as Calais had to be made.   She, poor woman, never once took up her veil.   There he sat, without closing an eye, stiff as a ramrod, sometimes showing by little uneasy gestures that the trouble at his neck was still there, but never speaking a word, and hardly moving a limb.

Crossing from Calais to Dover the lady was, of course, separated from her victim.   The passage was very bad, and she more than once reminded her husband how well it would have been with them now had they pursued their journey as she had intended — as though they had been detained in Paris by his fault!   Mr. Jones, as he laid himself down on his back, gave himself up to wondering whe.' . ny man before him had ever been made subject to such absolute injustice.   Now and again he put his hand up to his own beard, and began to doubt whether it could have been moved, as it must have been moved, without waking him.   What

if chloroform had been used? Many such sus-
picions crossed his mind during the misery of
that passage.

They were again together in the same railway carriage from Dover to London. They
had now got used to the close neighborhood,
and knew how to endure each the presence of
the other. But as yet Mr. Jones had never
seen the lady's face. He longed to know what
were the features of the woman who had been
so blind — if indeed that story were true. Or
if it were not true, of what like was the woman
who would dare in the middle of the night to
play such a trick as that? But still she kept
her veil close over her face.

From Cannon Street the Browns took their
departure in a cab for the Liverpool Street Station, whence they would be conveyed by the
Eastern Counties Railway to Stratford. Now,
at any rate, their troubles were over. They
would be in ample time not only for Christmas-
day church, but for Christmas-day breakfast.
" It will be just the same as getting in there
last night," said Mr. Brown, as he walked across
the platform to place his wife in the carriage
for Stratford. She entered it the first, and as
she did so, there she saw Mr. Jones seated in

the corner! Hitherto she had borne his presence well, but now she could not restrain herself from a little start and a little scream. He bowed his head very slightly, as though acknowledging the compliment, and then down she dropped her veil. When they arrived at Stratford, the journey being over in a quarter of an hour, Jones was out of the carriage even before the Browns.

"There is Uncle John's carriage," said Mrs. Brown, thinking that now, at any rate, she would be able to free herself from the presence of this terrible stranger. No doubt he was a handsome man to look at, but on no face so sternly hostile had she ever before fixed her eyes. She did not, perhaps, reflect that the owner of no other face had ever been so deeply injured by herself.

CHAPTER V.

MRS. BROWN AT THOMPSON HALL.

"PLEASE, sir, we were to ask for Mr. Jones," said the servant, putting his head into the carriage after both Mr. and Mrs. Brown had seated themselves.

" Mr. Jones!" exclaimed the husband.

"Why ask for Mr. Jones?" demanded the wife. The servant was about to tender some explanation, when Mr. Jones stepped up and said that he was Mr. Jones. "We are going to Thompson Hall," said the lady, with great vigor.

" So am I," said Mr. Jones, with much dignity. It was, however, arranged that he should sit with the coachman, as there was a rumble behind for the other servant. The luggage was put into a cart, and away all went for Thompson Hall.

"What do you think about it, Mary?" whispered Mr. Brown, after a pause. He was evidently awe-struck by the horror of the occasion.

" I cannot make it out at all. What do you think?"

"I don't know what to think. Jones going to Thompson Hall!"

"He's a very good-looking young man," said Mrs. Brown.

"Well—that's as people think. A stiff, stuck-up fellow, I should say. Up to this moment he has never forgiven you for what you did to him."

"Would you have forgiven his wife, Charles, if she'd done it to you?"

"He hasn't got a wife—yet."

"How do you know?"

"He is coming home now to be married," said Mr. Brown. "He expects to meet the young lady this very Christmas-day. He told me so. That was one of the reasons why he was so angry at being stopped by what you did last night."

"I suppose he knows Uncle John, or he wouldn't be going to the Hall," said Mrs. Brown.

"I can't make it out," said Mr. Brown, shaking his head.

"He looks quite like a gentleman," said Mrs. Brown, "though he has been so stiff. Jones! Barnaby Jones! You're sure it was Barnaby?"

"That was the name on the card."

"Not Burnaby?" asked Mrs. Brown.

"It was Barnaby Jones on the card— just the same as 'Barnaby Rudge'; and as for looking like a gentleman, I'm by no means quite so sure. A gentleman takes an apology when it's offered."

"Perhaps, my dear, that depends on the condition of his throat. If you had had a mustard plaster on all night, you might not have liked it. But here we are at Thompson Hall at last."

Thompson Hall was an old brick mansion, standing within a huge iron gate, with a gravel sweep before it. It had stood there before Stratford was a town, or even a suburb, and had then been known by the name of Bow Place. But it had been in the hands of the present family for the last thirty years, and was now known far and wide as Thompson Hall—a comfortable, roomy, old-fashioned place, perhaps a

little dark and dull to look at, but much more
substantially built than most of our modern
villas. Mrs. Brown jumped with alacrity from
the carriage, and with a quick step entered
the home of her forefathers. Her husband followed her more leisurely; but he too felt that
he was at home at Thompson Hall. Then Mr.
Jones walked in also; but he looked as though
he were not at all at home. It was still very
early, and no one of the family was as yet
down. In these circumstances it was almost
necessary that something should be said to Mr.
Jones.

"Do you know Mr. Thompson?" asked Mr.
Brown.

"I never had the pleasure of seeing him —
as yet," answered Mr. Jones, very stiffly.

"Oh — I didn't know. Because you said
you were coming here."

"And I have come here. Are you friends
of Mr. Thompson?"

"Oh dear yes," said Mrs. Brown. "I was a
Thompson myself before I married."

"Oh — indeed!" said Mr. Jones. "How very
odd! — very odd indeed."

During this time the luggage was being
brought into the house, and two old family

servants were offering them assistance. Would the new-comers like to go up to their bed-rooms? Then the housekeeper, Mrs. Green, intimated with a wink that Miss Jane would, she was sure, be down quite immediately. The present moment, however, was still very un-pleasant. The lady probably had made her guess as to the mystery, but the two gentlemen were still altogether in the dark. Mrs. Brown had no doubt declared her parentage, but Mr. Jones, with such a multitude of strange facts crowding on his mind, had been slow to un-derstand her. Being somewhat suspicious by nature, he was beginning to think whether pos-sibly the mustard had been put by this lady on his throat with some reference to his con-nection with Thompson Hall. Could it be that she, for some reason of her own, had wished to prevent his coming, and had contrived this un-toward stratagem out of her brain? or had she wished to make him ridiculous to the Thomp-son family, to whom, as a family, he was at present unknown? It was becoming more and more improbable to him that the whole thing should have been an accident. When, after the first horrid torments of that morning in which he had in his agony invoked the assistance of

the night porter, he had begun to reflect on his
situation, he had determined that it would be
better that nothing further should be said about
it.   What would life be worth to him if he were
to be known wherever he went as the man who
had been mustard-plastered in the middle of
the night by a strange lady?   The worst of a
practical joke is that the remembrance of the
absurd condition sticks so long to the sufferer.
At the hotel that night porter, who had possessed himself of the handkerchief, and had
read the name, and had connected that name
with the occupant of 333, whom he had found
wandering about the house with some strange
purpose, had not permitted the thing to sleep.
The porter had pressed the matter home against
the Browns, and had produced the interview
which has been recorded.   But during the
whole of that day Mr. Jones had been resolving
that he would never again either think of the
Browns or speak of them.   A great injury had
been done to him — a most outrageous injustice; but it was a thing which had to be en-
dured.   A horrid woman had come across him
like a nightmare.   All he could do was to
endeavor to forget the terrible visitation.   Such
had been his resolve, in making which he had

passed that long day in Paris. And now the
Browns had stuck to him from the moment of
his leaving his room! He had been forced to
travel with them, but had travelled with them
as a stranger. He had tried to comfort himself with the reflection that at every fresh stage
he would shake them off. In one railway after
another the vicinity had been bad — but still
they were strangers. Now he found himself in
the same house with them, where of course the
story would be told. Had not the thing been
done on purpose that the story might be told
there at Thompson Hall?

Mrs. Brown had acceded to the proposition
of the housekeeper, and was about to be taken
to her room, when there was heard a sound of
footsteps along the passage above and on the
stairs, and a young lady came bounding on to
the scene. "You have all of you come a
quarter of an hour earlier than we thought possible," said the young lady. "I did so mean
to be up to receive you!" With that she
passed her sister on the stairs — for the young
lady was Miss Jane Thompson, sister to our
Mrs. Brown — and hurried down into the hall.
Here Mr. Brown, who had ever been on affec-
tionate terms with his sister-in-law, put himself

forward to receive her embraces; but she, apparently not noticing him in her ardor, rushed on and threw herself on to the breast of the other gentleman. "This is my Charles," she said. "O Charles, I thought you never would be here!"

Mr. Charles Burnaby Jones — for such was his name since he had inherited the Jones property in Pembrokeshire — received into his arms the ardent girl of his heart with all that love and devotion to which she was entitled, but could not do so without some external shrinking from her embrace. "O Charles, what is it?" she said.

"Nothing, dearest — only — only —" Then he looked piteously up into Mrs. Brown's face, as though imploring her not to tell the story.

"Perhaps, Jane, you had better introduce us," said Mrs. Brown.

"Introduce you! I thought you had been travelling together, and staying at the same hotel, and all that."

"So we have; but people may be in the same hotel without knowing each other. And we have travelled all the way home with Mr. Jones without in the least knowing who he was."

"How very odd! Do you mean you have never spoken?"

"Not a word," said Mrs. Brown.

"I do so hope you'll love each other," said Jane.

"It sha'n't be my fault if we don't," said Mrs. Brown.

"I'm sure it sha'n't be mine," said Mr. Brown, tendering his hand to the other gentleman. The various feelings of the moment were too much for Mr. Jones, and he could not respond quite as he should have done. But as he was taken up-stairs to his room, he determined that he would make the best of it.

The owner of the house was old Uncle John. He was a bachelor, and with him lived various members of the family. There was the great Thompson of them all, Cousin Robert, who was now member of Parliament for the Essex Flats; and young John, as a certain enterprising Thompson of the age of forty was usually called; and then there was old Aunt Bess; and among other young branches there was Miss Jane Thompson, who was now engaged to marry Mr. Charles Burnaby Jones. As it happened, no other member of the family had as yet seen Mr. Burnaby Jones, and he, being by nature of a

retiring disposition, felt himself to be ill at ease
when he came into the breakfast parlor among
all the Thompsons.   He was known to be a
gentleman of good family and ample means,
and all the Thompsons had approved of the
match; but during that first Christmas breakfast he did not seem to accept his condition
jovially.   His own Jane sat beside him, but
then on the other side sat Mrs. Brown.   She
assumed an immediate intimacy — as women
know how to do on such occasions — being determined from the very first to regard her sister's husband as a brother; but he still feared
her.   She was still to him the woman who had
come to him in the dead of night with that horrid mixture — and had then left him.

"It was so odd that both of you should have
been detained on the very same day," said Jane.

"Yes, it was odd," said Mrs. Brown, with a
smile, looking round upon her neighbor.

"It was abominably bad weather, you know,"
said Brown.

"But you were both so determined to come,"
said the old gentleman. "When we got the two
telegrams at the same moment, we were sure
that there had been some agreement between
you."

"Not exactly an agreement," said Mrs. Brown; whereupon Mr. Jones looked as grim as death.

"I'm sure there is something more than we understand yet," said the member of Parliament.

Then they all went to church, as a united family ought to do on Christmas-day, and came home to a fine old English early dinner at three o'clock, — a sirloin of beef a foot and a half broad, a turkey as big as an ostrich, a plum-pudding bigger than the turkey,  and two or three dozen mince-pies. "That's a very large bit of beef," said Mr. Jones, who had not lived much in England latterly.

"It won't look so large," said the old gentleman, "when all our friends down-stairs have had their say to it." "A plum pudding on Christmas-day can't be too big," he said again, "if the cook will but take time enough over it. I never knew a bit to go to waste yet."

By this time there had been some explanation as to past events between the two sisters. Mrs. Brown had, indeed, told Jane all about it, — how ill her husband had been, how she had been forced to go down and look for the mustard, and then what she had done with the mustard.

"I don't think they are a bit alike, you know, Mary, if you mean that," said Jane.

"Well, no; perhaps not quite alike. I only saw his beard, you know. No doubt it was stupid, but I did it."

"Why didn't you take it off again?" asked the sister.

"O Jane, if you'd only think of it! Could you?" Then, of course, all that occurred was explained,— how they had been stopped on their journey, how Brown had made the best apology in his power, and how Jones had travelled with them and had never spoken a word. The gentleman had only taken his new name a week since, but of course had had his new card printed immediately. "I'm sure I should have thought of it, if they hadn't made a mistake of the first name. Charles said it was like Barnaby Rudge."

"Not at all like Barnaby Rudge," said Jane: "Charles Burnaby Jones is a very good name."

"Very good indeed — and I'm sure that after a little bit he won't be at all the worse for the accident."

Before dinner the secret had been told no further, but still there had crept about among the Thompsons, and, indeed, down-stairs also among the retainers, a feeling that there was a secret. The old housekeeper was sure that Miss Mary, as she still called Mrs. Brown, had something to tell, if she could only be induced to tell it, and that this something had reference to Mr. Jones's personal comfort. The head of the family, who was a sharp old gentleman, felt this also, and the member of Parliament, who had an idea that he especially should never be kept in the dark, was almost angry. Mr. Jones, suffering from some kindred feeling throughout the dinner, remained silent and unhappy. When two or three toasts had been drunk — the Queen's health, the old gentleman's health, the young couple's health, Brown's health, and the general health of all the Thompsons — then tongues were loosened and a question was asked. "I know that there has been something doing in Paris between these young people that we haven't heard as yet," said the uncle. Then Mrs. Brown laughed, and Jane, laughing too, gave Mr. Jones to understand that she, at any rate, knew all about it.

"If there is a mystery, I hope it will be told at once," said the member of Parliament angrily.

"Come, Brown, what is it?" asked another male cousin.

"Well, there was an accident. I'd rather Jones should tell," said he.

Jones's brow became blacker than thunder, but he did not say a word. "You mustn't be angry with Mary," Jane whispered into her lover's ear.

"Come, Mary, you never were slow at talking," said the uncle.

"I do hate this kind of thing," said the member of Parliament.

"I will tell it all," said Mrs. Brown, very nearly in tears, or else pretending to be very nearly in tears. "I know I was very wrong, and I do beg his pardon; and if he won't say that he forgives me, I never shall be happy again." Then she clasped her hands, and, turning round, looked him piteously in the face.

"Oh, yes; I do forgive you," said Mr. Jones.

"My brother," said she, throwing her arms round him and kissing him. He recoiled from the embrace, but I think that he attempted to return the kiss. "And now I will tell the whole story," said Mrs. Brown. And she told it, acknowledging her fault with true contrition, and swearing that she would atone for it by life-long sisterly devotion.

"And you mustard-plastered the wrong man!" said the old gentleman, almost rolling off his chair with delight.

"I did," said Mrs. Brown, sobbing; "and I think that no woman ever suffered as I suffered."

"And Jones wouldn't let you leave the hotel?"

"It was the handkerchief stopped us," said Brown.

"If it had turned out to be anybody else," said the member of Parliament, "the results might have been most serious— not to say discreditable."

"That's nonsense, Robert," said Mrs. Brown, who was disposed to resent the use of so severe a word, even from the legislator cousin.

"In a strange gentleman's bedroom!" he continued. "It only shows that what I have always said is quite true. You should never go to bed in a strange house without locking your door."

Nevertheless it was a very jovial meeting and before the evening was over Mr. Jones was happy, and had been brought to acknowledge that the mustard plaster would probably not do him any permanent injury.

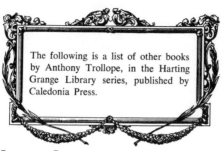

The following is a list of other books by Anthony Trollope, in the Harting Grange Library series, published by Caledonia Press.

THE LADY OF LAUNAY

Mrs. Miles, the Lady of Launay, is a widow "possessed of wealth and social position." Martyrly she denies herself all delights, especially the delights of money and society. But what she will not deny herself is her own "idea of duty." For that idea she would turn her son out of her house; and she would force her ward Bessy Pryor to marry a man she cannot love.

ISBN 0-932282-02-4 (softcover)
ISBN 0-932282-03-2 (library binding)

WHY FRAU FROHMANN RAISED HER PRICES

"There you come to people with fixed incomes," said Mr. Cartwright, an Englishman in this novel: "The few who live upon what they have saved or others have saved for them must go to the wall."

This novel, written in 1877, is frankly about inflation and what it does to people.

ISBN 0-932282-05-9 (softcover)
ISBN 0-932282-06-7 (library binding)

CHRISTMAS AT THOMPSON HALL

A Mid-Victorian Christmas tale, in the tradition of Charles Dickens, but with Trollope's unique sense of affection, understanding and humor.

ISBN 0-932282-07-5 (hardcover trade)
ISBN 0-932282-08-3 (softcover)
ISBN 0-932282-09-1 (library binding)

ALICE DUGDALE

Alice Dugdale is one of Trollope's most intelligent and modern heroines. The problem is Major Rossiter doesn't know if he wants a girl intelligent and strong, or if he prefers one beautiful and fashionable and dull.

ISBN 0-932282-11-3 (softcover)
ISBN 0-932282-12-1 (library binding)

TRAVEL SKETCHES

A volume where the chapter-titles indicate the topics and treatment of the book. I. The Family that goes abroad because it's the thing to do. II. The man who travels alone. III. The unprotected female tourist. IV. The united Englishmen who travel for fun. V. The art tourist. VI. The tourist in search of knowledge. VII. The Alpine club man. VIII. Tourists who don't like their travels.

ISBN 0-932282-15-6 (softcover)
ISBN 0-932282-16-4 (library binding)

MARION FAY

The Reverend Thomas Greenwood is the domestic chaplain and private secretary to the Marquess of Kingbury. He is stout, self-indulgent and ambitious: he meditates upon the murder of his patron's eldest son and heir. A dark, gothic, unsparing novel.

ISBN 0-932282-18-0 (softcover)
ISBN 0-932282-19-9 (library binding)

Consult your bookseller for details or write Caledonia Press for a descriptive catalog.

Caledonia Press
P.O. Box 245
Racine, Wisconsin
53401 U.S.A.